Wish Upon a Song

It's a wish come true! Read all the
books in the Lucky Stars series:

Wish Upon a Song

by Phoebe Bright
illustrated by Karen Donnelly

SCHOLASTIC INC.
NEW YORK   TORONTO   LONDON   AUCKLAND
SYDNEY   MEXICO CITY   NEW DELHI   HONG KONG

With thanks to all the magical people
in my life for their belief in me

Special thanks to Maria Faulkner

ISBN 978-0-545-42000-6

12 11 10 9 8 7 6 5 4 3 2 1   12 13 14 15 16 17/0

Printed in the China   68
First Scholastic printing, September 2012

Lucky Star that shines so bright,
Who will need your help tonight?
Light up the sky, and thanks to you
Wishes really do come true. . . .

Hello, friend!

I'm Stella Starkeeper, and I want to tell you a secret. Have you ever gazed up at the stars and thought that they could be full of magic? Well, you're right. Stars really are magical!

Their precious starlight allows me to fly down from the sky. I'm always on the lookout for boys and girls who are especially kind and helpful. I train them to become Lucky Stars—people who can make wishes come true!

So the next time you're under the twinkling night sky, look out for me. I'll be floating among the stars somewhere.

Give me a wave!

Love,

Stella Starkeeper

1
Songs on the Sand

"Magic moments, these are magic moments . . ." Cassie sang.

"Yowl, yowl, meow, yowl . . ." her black-and-white cat, Twinkle, joined in.

Their voices echoed in the huge observatory dome at Starwatcher Towers. Cassie was singing along to "Magic Moments," the latest hit by Jacey Day. She was Cassie's favorite pop star! In fact, that afternoon Cassie and her friend Kate were going to watch Jacey perform. She was the opening act in the Songs on the Sand music festival, right in their own town of Astral-on-Sea!

All week, Cassie and Kate had been practicing a special dance routine to "Magic Moments." As she twirled around, Cassie imagined that Kate was also dancing in the Fairy Cupcake Bakery, the store that her mom owned.

Cassie turned up the music. "Let's dance, Twinkle!" she said with a giggle.

Her old cat blinked his eyes. Cassie scooped him up from the old leather chair where he sat, and spun around, being careful not to bump into any of the shiny telescopes. Her dad was an astronomer. Most nights, he could be found up here in the observatory, studying the stars.

"There's a friend I'd love to meet,
Spinning world beneath his feet.
He's got pebbles in his hands,
Running 'cross the glistening sands. . . ."

Along with Jacey's sweet, clear voice, the backup singers added a catchy harmony to the song. The sound of their voices blending together made Cassie want to sing and dance!

When the song ended, Cassie noticed a tingling feeling on her arm. She put Twinkle back on the chair and looked at the charm bracelet around her wrist. Her new butterfly charm seemed to flutter its colorful wings.

"I wonder what magical power this charm has," Cassie said, "and who I'll help next."

Cassie used her charms to help make people's wishes come true! With each person she helped, she received another magic charm for her bracelet. So far, Cassie had three. The bird charm gave her the power to fly, and the crescent moon allowed her to talk to animals. But she still wasn't sure what the butterfly charm did. She couldn't wait to find out!

"Meow!" Twinkle's ears twitched. He seemed to be trying to tell her something.

Cassie concentrated hard on her crescent moon charm, so its magic could help her understand him. "What is it, Twinkle?" she asked.

"I can hear music," he said. His ears twitched again. "It's coming from outside."

Cassie listened. Yes, there *was* music! She gazed up into the bright blue sky and saw a star shining there. Cassie knew that it was unusual to see a star in daylight, but she also knew this was no ordinary star.

As she watched, the star zoomed straight through the open skylight of the dome, filling the observatory with beautiful music. Then, with a *whizz* and a *fizz* and a *zip-zip-zip*, it landed next to Cassie.

"Meow!" Twinkle darted under the chair and covered his eyes with his paws.

But Cassie watched with delight as the star grew into a column of dazzling light, which slowly changed into . . .

"Stella Starkeeper!" Cassie flung her arms around her friend. "It's so good to see you!"

Stella was helping Cassie become a Lucky Star. Today she looked as pretty as ever. Her silver dress and leggings glittered above her shiny boots, and her long silver-blonde hair

rippled over her shoulders.

"I see you've earned your third charm," Stella said. "Good work, Cassie! Soon you'll have all seven charms, and can become a Lucky Star. Then you'll be able to grant wishes whenever you want!"

"I can't wait," said Cassie. She turned the little butterfly charm in her fingers and looked at its pretty pink wings. "But what does my new charm do?"

Twinkle creeped out from under the chair and tried to bat at the charm with his paw.

Stella laughed and tickled Twinkle under the chin, making him purr loudly. "I'll give you a clue," she said, her blue eyes shining. "You have all the time in the world to figure it out. . . ."

Beautiful music filled the dome again. With a wave, Stella disappeared in a shower of glittering sparkles.

Cassie looked at Twinkle. *"All the time in the world.* I wonder what Stella meant?"

2
Mystery Guests

Cassie ran downstairs to the first floor, jumping over the bottom three steps. At the same moment, her mom came out of the kitchen carrying a tray with a jug of water, some freshly baked cookies, and a vase of flowers. Cassie stopped just in time — one more step and they would have crashed!

"Careful, Cass," said Mom. "You almost flew right into me!"

Cassie smiled to herself. Good thing she

hadn't used her bird charm to *really* fly down the stairs!

"Sorry, Mom," she said, holding the dining room door open and waving to her dad inside.

"I heard you singing and dancing," Cassie's dad said with a grin. "Are you sure Jacey Day wasn't up there with you?"

Cassie giggled and looked at the dining table that her dad was polishing. Her brown eyes and blonde hair were reflected in its gleaming surface. "Wow, it's as shiny as a mirror!" she said.

"We're getting ready for some surprise guests," Dad explained. "The reservation just came through this morning."

Starwatcher Towers wasn't just an

observatory—it was a bed-and-breakfast, too! Cassie's mom ran the B&B, and her dad used the observatory for his astronomy work.

"The travel agent acted like it was some sort of big secret," said Mom. "All they told us is that the guests are a mom and daughter who need lots of privacy."

"We don't even know their names!" Dad added.

Cassie raised her eyebrows. "Very mysterious," she said, wondering who the guests could be.

"All mysteries can be solved, as long as you carefully examine the facts," said a familiar voice behind her.

Cassie turned to see Alex standing in the hallway with his little white puppy, Comet. She grinned at them. Alex and his parents were staying at the B&B on vacation. He was obsessed with science! At first, he hadn't believed in Stella Starkeeper or Cassie's magical bracelet. But soon he changed his mind, and he and Cassie had become good friends.

Ring-ring! Ring-ring!

"*Ruff! Ruff!*" Comet leaped around the

hallway, barking at the ringing telephone.

"Sit, Comet. Good boy," Alex said, petting his excited puppy.

Comet flopped down, wagging his tail, as Cassie's mom answered the phone.

"Hello—Starwatcher Towers. Can I help you?" Cassie's mom said. "Oh, hi!" She paused, her smile turning into a worried frown. "Oh, no. Yes, of course I'll tell Cassie. I hope Kate will feel better soon."

"What's wrong with Kate?" Cassie asked as soon as her mom hung up. "She can still go to the concert, right?"

Cassie's mom shook her head. "I'm afraid not. Her mom says she's in bed with a sore throat."

"Poor Kate! She must be so disappointed that she'll miss seeing Jacey Day." Cassie gave a heavy sigh. "Our song and dance routine was almost perfect."

"I know," Mom said, giving Cassie a hug.

"You'll just have to sing twice as loud now. And maybe you could do something nice to cheer up Kate."

Cassie nodded, but she couldn't help feeling disappointed.

Comet ran over and licked Cassie's toes, as if he was trying to make her feel better. Cassie smiled.

"I think Comet wants to go to the concert with you," Alex said, laughing.

Suddenly, Cassie had an idea!

"Would *you* like to go to the concert with me, Alex?" she asked him hopefully. "I have the tickets already."

Ss **Songs** **on the** **Sand**

"Really?" Alex's brown eyes lit up. "I'd love to! I've never been to a concert before, so it'll be kind of like a science experiment for me."

Cassie giggled and did a little twirl down the hallway. Alex grinned.

Ding-dong! The doorbell echoed in the hallway. Mom hurried to answer it. "Looks like our mystery guests have arrived," she said.

Cassie felt a flutter of excitement. *Who could they be?*

"Hello," Cassie's mom said to the tall, thin woman standing on the doorstep. "Welcome to Starwatcher Towers."

Behind her, Cassie could see a girl with long, dark hair. She was wearing sunglasses, skinny jeans, a cropped pink jacket, and glittery silver sneakers. Cassie smiled at her, and the girl waved back.

"It's so nice to be here," the woman said. "My daughter and I have had a long trip."

"Please come in and make yourselves right at home," Mom said, holding the door open.

The woman smiled at Cassie as she walked past in her high heels, leaving a faint whiff of perfume behind her. Dad helped carry in their suitcases, which looked awfully fancy to Cassie.

Outside, the girl had wandered onto the lawn and was speaking quietly into her cell phone.

"Wow," Cassie whispered to Alex. "She looks like a movie star with those big sunglasses."

"I think she must be a famous scientist," Alex replied. "See that phone? It's very high-tech. It can do all sorts of things!"

"I love her shiny hair," Cassie said with a little sigh. "And her silver sneakers. Our mystery guests are so fancy!"

Alex adjusted his glasses, trying to get a better look. "Really?" he said. "Their clothes look pretty normal to me."

Cassie grinned. Alex would only notice someone's outfit if it were a lab coat and science goggles!

Cassie knew it wasn't polite to stare, but she couldn't seem to tear her eyes away from the girl. Even though she couldn't see much of the girl's face behind those big sunglasses, Cassie was sure she had seen her somewhere before. But where?

3
Jacey Day!

Cassie and Alex watched from the front step as the girl finished her call and glanced at the gold watch on her wrist. She walked back and forth across the lawn, her forehead creased with worry.

"I wonder what's wrong?" said Cassie quietly.

"It looks like she just got some bad news," said Alex. "Maybe she's the person you're supposed to help."

Cassie shook her head. "She's so glamorous. She doesn't need *me* to make her wish come true!"

At last, the girl walked over to Cassie and Alex. "Hi," she said with a grin.

"Hi," Cassie replied, suddenly feeling shy. "I'm Cassie, and this is Alex."

"Um . . . hello," said Alex.

"It's very nice to meet you," the girl said. But to Cassie's surprise, she didn't tell them her name. Instead, she pointed to Cassie's wrist. "I like your charm bracelet. I've never seen one like it before."

"Thank you!" Cassie jingled her bracelet and smiled. The girl couldn't possibly know how special it really was!

"I—um—heard about the Songs on the

Sand festival that's
going on today. Do
you know how to get
there?" the girl asked.

"Alex and I can show
you the way to the beach,"
Cassie said. "We'll be
going there ourselves
soon."

"Do you have a
ticket?" Alex asked
the girl.

"Don't worry," she said.
"I won't need a ticket."

Cassie and Alex
exchanged a surprised
look. Why wouldn't the

girl need a ticket? *Whoever she is*, Cassie thought, *she's very mysterious. . . .*

★ ★ ★

Cassie, Alex, and the girl arranged to meet their parents at the festival and headed for the beach. Comet bounded along next to them.

Cassie pointed at a cluster of tents in the distance. "You can see the festival from here," she said as they walked down the hill.

"There's a carnival, too!" Alex said before Comet tugged on his leash, pulling Alex ahead of the two girls.

"You seem so familiar," Cassie told the other girl. "I'm sure I've seen you before."

The girl didn't reply, but pushed her sunglasses farther up the bridge of her nose.

"Sorry, I don't think I got your name," Cassie said, feeling more curious about this visitor by the minute.

"Oh, right . . . I'm Jacinta," the girl replied. "Thanks for showing me to the festival."

Alex ran back toward them. "Look at that crowd!" he said. He thought for a minute. "I estimate that there must be at least a thousand people!"

They all ran down the last part of the

hill and onto the boardwalk. Cassie felt her heart pound with excitement—she would be seeing Jacey Day perform soon! She started to sing "Magic Moments."

"When the city's far away,
Then the sunshine fills my day. . . ."

Jacinta gave her a curious smile. "That's a Jacey Day song," she said.

"Yes, she's the best," Cassie said. "I can't wait to see her in concert today!"

Cassie noticed that Jacinta's forehead had creased up with worry again. What was bothering her?

As they hurried along the boardwalk, Cassie waved to Bert, who was giving donkey rides to kids on the beach. When they finally reached the festival gates, they spotted a huge billboard that showed the list of singers and when they were set to perform. Jacey Day's name was first.

"Look," Cassie said pointing at the billboard. "Perfect timing — Jacey's on soon!"

Jacinta just nodded, looking even more worried than before.

What could be the matter? Cassie wondered. *I don't know how to help unless I can find out what's wrong.* An official-looking man carrying a clipboard walked up to the gates. As he approached, he spoke into a cell phone. Cassie noticed that Jacinta was tapping her foot anxiously.

"Yup," the man said. "I've found her. I'll let her know."

He beckoned for them to come through the gates. They didn't even have to show their tickets! What was going on?

"Have you found anyone else?" Jacinta asked the man in a quiet voice.

"No, I'm sorry. It's hard to find replacements with such short notice," he told her.

Jacinta's face fell. "But it will be a disaster without them," she said sadly. "Is there anything else you can do?"

"I wonder what's going to be a disaster,"

Cassie whispered to Alex. "And how does she know this guy?" Alex shrugged, looking confused.

The man spoke into his phone, waited for an answer, and then shook his head.

"Sorry, there's no chance," he said to Jacinta. "I'm afraid you'll have to do it on your own or cancel."

Cancel what? thought Cassie.

Jacinta turned away and covered her face with her hands. Tears were trickling down her cheeks.

"Oh, please don't cry!" Cassie exclaimed. She pulled a tissue from her pocket and offered it to Jacinta.

"Thanks," Jacinta said, sniffling. She took off her sunglasses and wiped the tears from her eyes.

Just then, Cassie's heart did a flip-flop of excitement.

She couldn't believe it. Jacinta was actually Jacey Day!

4
All the Time in the World

Still clutching the crumpled tissue, Jacey slipped her sunglasses back on before anyone else recognized her.

"Oh, of course!" Alex said, hopping up and down with excitement. "Jacey must be short for Jacinta. Wow, I've never met a famous person before!"

Cassie could barely contain herself. She had so many questions she wanted to ask Jacey! What was her favorite color? Did she have any pets?

"I can't believe
you're staying with us!"
she cried. "Starwatcher
Towers is only a little
bed-and-breakfast. Why
aren't you staying at a
fancy hotel like Flashley
Manor?"

"I liked the name," Jacey replied. "And it's
so cool that it's an observatory, too. Anyway,
it gets hard at the big hotels where there are
so many people. Mom thought it would be a
good idea to try a place where I'd attract less
attention."

She smiled at Cassie, but then looked sad
again as a boy and girl walked past. They

were wearing "WE LOVE JACEY" T-shirts, and were too busy talking to notice that Jacey was standing right there!

"Jacey Day's on soon," the boy was saying. "We'd better hurry."

Jacey looked at her watch. "Oh, no! We're out of time. Everyone who came to see me perform is going to be so disappointed."

"Why?" Cassie asked. "What happened?"

"My backup singers called earlier to say that they both had sore throats and weren't sure if they could sing," Jacey explained. "The

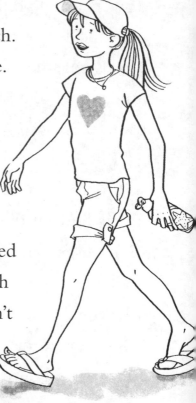

man with the clipboard is the festival manager. He heard that they're definitely too sick to come, and he hasn't been able to find replacements."

They're sick, just like Kate, Cassie thought.

"I'm so upset," Jacey continued. "All summer I've been looking forward to Songs on the Sand. This is such a beautiful place, and it almost seems like 'Magic Moments' was made for Astral-on-Sea."

"Isn't there anything we can do?" asked Cassie. "Maybe Alex and I can help."

"I don't think so, but thanks." Jacey gave a deep sigh. "You've heard the song. I sing the melody, but it won't work without the backup singers."

Cassie thought back to being in the

observatory, singing and dancing with Twinkle. She knew that Jacey was right.

"My fans will be so disappointed if I don't sing my hit song," said Jacey, frowning. "I really wish I could perform 'Magic Moments' here."

Cassie and Alex glanced at each other. Jacey had made a wish — to sing "Magic Moments" at the Songs on the Sand festival! Cassie couldn't believe it. So Jacey Day really *did* need her help! But how could she make her wish come true?

Cassie looked at her charm bracelet glittering in the sunlight. Her new butterfly charm spun slowly in the breeze. She had to figure out what the charm could do.

"I have an idea," Cassie said. "We could stage auditions! There are plenty of people here, so there's bound to be someone who can sing 'Magic Moments' with you."

Jacey glanced at her watch. "Backup singers would need all the time in the world to learn the harmonies, and I'm supposed to go onstage in a few minutes. I might have to cancel."

Cassie gasped. Wait! What had Jacey just said? *All the time in the world . . .*

She could guess now what Stella Starkeeper's clue had meant—and she knew the magical power of her new charm!

Gazing at the tiny butterfly, Cassie concentrated hard. The charm sparkled brightly, and the tiny wings flapped—one-two, one-two, just like the ticking hands of a clock.

All around her people stopped, standing as still as statues. A seagull froze mid-flight. In the ice-cream line, a boy who was making funny faces was now stuck with his tongue

out! Comet stood on his hind legs with his front paws in the air, tail frozen mid-wag. Cassie realized that it was like pressing the pause button on her DVD player. Nothing moved. Everything was still and silent.

Amazing, thought Cassie. *Now I really can make Jacey's wish come true. I have all the time in the world!*

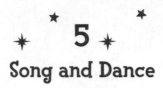

5
Song and Dance

Jacey and Alex were also frozen in front of Cassie. Jacey's forehead was puckered with worry, and Alex had his mouth open, as if he was about to speak.

Oh, no, Cassie thought. *How do I unfreeze Alex and no one else?*

She had an idea, so she put her hand on his arm. "I'm going to need your help, Alex," she said. "I wish you would wake up!"

Immediately, Alex came to life.

"Whoa!" he cried, staring around at the still, silent crowd of people. "What happened?"

"It's my butterfly charm," said Cassie. "It gives me the power to freeze time."

Alex shook his head in disbelief. "But that's not scientifically possible."

"It's not science," Cassie reminded him. "It's magic."

She leaned down and touched Comet on the top of his furry head. "I wish you would wake up too, Comet."

The little puppy immediately wagged his tail. *"Ruff!"* he barked in surprise.

"Come on, follow me!" Cassie said to Alex. "I have an idea."

They left Jacey standing frozen to the spot and ran toward the fairground stalls. "We need some costumes," said Cassie.

"Costumes?" echoed Alex. "What for?"

"You'll see," answered Cassie, plonking a big straw hat with the Songs on the Sand logo on his head. As they reached the stalls, she put one on, too, then added a pair of sparkly sunglasses and looked in the stall's mirror.

Alex straightened the hat and tried on a pair of sunglasses with bright blue lenses. "What do you think?"

"Perfect!" said Cassie.

Pulling out her purse, she left some money

at the stand. Then she ran up a flight of wooden steps that led to the area behind the stage. There, they found big spotlights, speakers, and frozen festival organizers.

Cassie stashed the hats and sunglasses behind a woman wearing headphones, then ran back to where Jacey was still standing, frozen.

"Okay," Cassie said, turning to Alex. "We have a lot of practicing to do if we're going to be Jacey's backup singers."

"We're going to sing? In front of all these people?" Alex gulped.

"Yes," Cassie said with a big grin. She looked around at the huge audience that had gathered to see the performance. "We're going to make Jacey's wish come true!"

Alex was quiet for a moment. Then he said, "But, Cassie, I don't even know the words to 'Magic Moments.' Besides, I like singing to myself in the bathtub, but I get scared in front of lots of people. I'll sound awful!"

Cassie's face fell. Maybe her plan wasn't going to work after all. She looked at Alex, nervously hopping from foot to foot, then at the frozen tears on Jacey's face.

"But we have to do it," she declared. "Don't worry, Alex. I'll teach you the words to 'Magic Moments.' Then we'll work on the rest. Please," she added. "I can't make Jacey's wish come true without you!"

"Then I'll give it a try," Alex said. "You're my friend, and I want to help."

Cassie grinned at Alex and started to sing:

"Kids are building castles high
With cotton candy and ice-cream smiles. . . ."

Alex listened. Then he tried to sing the words back to her:

"Kids are building candy high
With something, something and dreamy smiles. . . ."

He kept getting the lines wrong!

"Oh, no," Cassie said. "I don't think I'm teaching you very well."

She sat in one of the nearby chairs, next to a lady whose ice-cream drips were hovering in midair.

Alex slumped into the chair on her other side. "I'm sorry, Cassie. I can write out a complicated math problem off the top of my head, but I can't seem to remember the words to a song."

"That's it!" Cassie said, her eyes lighting up. "If I write down the words to the song, you'll remember them better. Do you have your notebook and pen with you?"

Alex pulled them out of his pocket and handed them over.

Cassie wrote down the words, and she and Alex practiced them over and over again. "That's much better," Cassie said once Alex had sung the words correctly all the way through. "Now we need to practice the harmonies together. But if I'm singing, too, I won't be able to tell if it sounds right."

Just then, Comet sat in front of them. He placed his chin on Alex's knee and his paw on Cassie's hand.

Alex grinned. "Let's ask Comet to help."

"Comet?" Cassie giggled, remembering Twinkle's singing earlier in the day. "But he's a puppy. He can't sing!"

They both looked at Comet. Ears raised, he wagged his tail, making his whole body wiggle. Cassie could tell that he thought something interesting was going on.

"That's true," Alex said. "He can't sing. But dogs do have special hearing — it's supersensitive. They can move their ears in different directions to pick up more sounds than we can."

"So Comet can tell us whether he thinks we sound good or not," said Cassie excitedly. "Great idea, Alex!"

6

Practice Makes Perfect

Cassie thought hard about her crescent moon charm, which gave her the power to talk to animals. Sparkles swirled from her charm bracelet and danced around Comet's head.

"Comet, we need your help," said Cassie.

"Hooray!" Comet yipped. "What do you want me to do?"

"We need you to listen to us sing 'Magic Moments.' Can you tell us how we sound

together, and if we're singing in tune?"
Cassie asked.

"No problem!" Comet replied.
He rushed around the
chairs, then leaped
onto one of them
and sat with his
ears straight up. "I'm
ready," he said.

Cassie laughed.
"Thanks, Comet."
She turned to Alex. "Let's try singing it
together—on the stage, this time."

They climbed up onto the stage. Cassie
weaved through the people setting up the
music equipment, who were all frozen in
place. Carefully, she took a microphone out

of its stand. Alex borrowed his microphone from a woman whose tinted glasses were almost falling off the end of her nose.

On the count of three, Cassie started to sing. *"Magic, magic moments . . ."*

"Good, Cassie," Comet barked from the front row. "But I can hardly hear Alex. He's mumbling."

"Alex, Comet says you need to sing louder," Cassie told him. "You've got to sing loudly enough for the people in the back row to hear you."

Alex looked down at his feet. "But it's scary singing to all these people," he said quietly.

Cassie thought for a minute. "You said you like singing to yourself in the bathtub, right?"

Alex nodded.

"Well, pretend you're
singing to yourself,
but in a great big
bathtub," said Cassie.
"The biggest tub in
the world!"

Alex laughed. They
started the song again,
and this time, Cassie could hear Alex's
singing get louder and louder as he became
more confident. Soon he was belting out his
lines, matching Cassie's soaring voice.

"Magic, magic moments,
These are magic moments. . . ."

"I never knew I could sing like that," Alex said with a big grin when they finished. "It's fun!"

"Well, I think you're really good," said Cassie. "Let's see what Comet thinks."

"Hooray!" barked the little puppy. "You both sounded fantastic!"

Cassie smiled. They were almost ready to start time again.

"Now we'll just add the dance steps," she told Alex.

"I'm really not very good at dancing," Alex said, gulping again. "But I guess I'll try. After all, until today I didn't think I was very good at singing, either."

Cassie grinned at Alex. He was trying so hard to be a good friend and to help make Jacey's wish come true!

Cassie danced around the band members, waving at the frozen drummer, who looked as if he were smiling at them. Alex followed, copying Cassie's routine. Then she noticed him adding his own moves.

"What do you think of this, Cassie?" he

said. "I'm calling it the sound wave." He did a rippling arm movement. "And this move is like a clock ticking." He hopped from foot to foot, rhythmically.

"I love it!" said Cassie, copying him.

They practiced the whole routine from the beginning again, adding in Alex's new moves. The frozen people in the audience looked like they were cheering them on. Cassie felt

her heart flutter when she imagined all those people actually listening to them.

"*. . . Magic moments in our lives!*"

They sang the final line of the song for the last time and took a bow. Cassie waved to the frozen Jacey. It was time to make her wish come true!

"Bravo!" Comet barked. "Now, how about a treat?"

Alex found a dog biscuit in his pocket and gave it to Comet as a thank-you for his help.

"All this practice is hard work. It's a good thing we had all the time in the world," said Cassie, jingling her bracelet. "But do you think we're ready to start time again, Alex?"

Alex nodded. "Ready."

Cassie looked at her butterfly charm and thought very hard. It sparkled, and the tiny pink wings fluttered again.

Immediately, everyone burst into life. Noise and movement erupted all around them. A group of older boys and girls danced next to their friend, who was playing a guitar. People pointed out the bands listed in the festival program and talked about who they wanted to see. The woman's ice-cream cone dripped onto the sand. Jacey wiped the tears from her eyes. Nothing had changed.

Except for one thing, Cassie thought.

"I hope Jacey thinks we're good enough," she whispered to Alex.

"Of course she will," Alex replied.

Cassie nodded. "Jacey," she said. "I think Alex and I can help you. We could be your backup singers for 'Magic Moments.' Come on, we'll show you."

When Cassie and Alex finished their demonstration for Jacey backstage, she clapped her hands and cheered.

"That was amazing! Cassie, your harmonies sound wonderful. And your dance

moves are so great, Alex,"
Jacey said, excited.
"Now what should
we do about
costumes?"

Cassie exchanged
a secret grin with
Alex. "We'll surprise
you!" she said.

"You already
have surprised me,"
Jacey said, giving
them both a big hug.
"Thank you so much.
You've come to the
rescue — and just
in time!"

The festival manager walked toward Jacey, pointing at his watch. "Sorry, Miss Day, but you're out of time. Should I tell them that your performance is canceled?"

"No! No need to cancel," Jacey said, a big smile lighting up her face. "We have a brand-new act. It might not be what the fans are expecting, but I know they're going to love it!"

Cassie felt a shiver of happiness. Not only was she going to make Jacey's wish come true—she was going to sing and dance with her, too! She couldn't wait to tell Kate and all her other friends. Some of them would even be in the crowd watching! *This is going to be my very own magic moment!* she thought.

7

Magic Moments

Backstage, Cassie and Alex put on the costumes that Cassie had hidden. The festival organizers bustled around them, putting the spotlights in position and testing the speaker system.

Jacey was standing near the stage entrance next to a man wearing a headset. She waved to Cassie and Alex.

When everything was ready, the man turned

to Jacey. "Three, two, one—go!" he said.

Jacey strode onto the stage and the audience broke into wild cheers. Cassie and Alex watched from the wings, standing on tiptoes so they could see what was happening.

Jacey held up her hands, and everyone quieted down.

"Thank you, Astral-on-Sea," Jacey said into the microphone, smiling. "I'm so happy to be opening the Songs on the

Sand music festival!"

Another roar from the crowd filled the air.

"I'd like to sing you a very special song. It makes me think about the wonderful time I'm having here," said Jacey. "It's called 'Magic Moments.'"

The audience cheered, then went quiet again as Jacey continued.

"As you know, I need my backup singers to sing the special harmony on this song, but they couldn't make it here today."

There was a disappointed sigh from the audience.

"However . . ." Jacey went on. She held out a hand as Cassie and Alex walked onto the stage, wearing their straw hats and big sunglasses. Jacey grinned at them.

"I'm so glad you're here," she whispered. Then she turned to the crowd. "Please welcome Cassie and Alex, my new backup singers. They're the Jacey Day Stars!"

The crowd cheered again, and Cassie and Alex smiled at each other. Cassie spotted her mom and dad near the front of the crowd. Their mouths were hanging wide open in astonishment at seeing her on the stage with Jacey! Alex's parents were next to them, looking surprised and clapping excitedly. Cassie waved and blew them all a kiss.

Before she knew it, the band began to play and Jacey started to sing.

"There's a friend I'd love to meet. . . ."

Cassie looked
at Alex and gave
him a nod. Then
they both joined
in, singing and
dancing with Jacey and
the band.

"Spinning world beneath his feet. . . ."

Their voices sounded great! The song seemed to fly by, and suddenly the last words hung in the air.

". . . Magic moments in our lives!"

On the final note, an explosion of shooting

stars, in violet, gold, orange, and scarlet, poured over the stage like a twinkling snowstorm. The crowd went wild.

"Where did that come from?" Jacey gasped.

Cassie smiled. She knew. *Stella Starkeeper.*

Jacey bowed, then beckoned to Cassie and Alex. Holding hands, they all bowed together. As they straightened up again, the festival manager walked onstage and gave them each

a beautiful bouquet of flowers. Cassie was so happy she thought she would burst.

Alex grinned at her. "That was incredible!" he whispered as they waved to the audience and left the stage.

"Better than singing in the bathtub?" Cassie teased.

While Jacey signed autographs, Cassie and Alex ran over to their parents.

"Congratulations," said Alex's mom, shaking her head in amazement. "You sounded really good."

"They were fantastic," Cassie's mom agreed.

"I never knew you could sing like that— you must take after me," said Alex's dad, winking at him.

"What I can't understand is when you had the time to practice," said Jacey's mom, walking over from where she had been watching in the wings. She hugged Cassie and Alex at the same time. "You two were magical."

The two friends exchanged a secret smile.

Just then, Cassie felt a tingling sensation on her wrist, and she looked down at her charm bracelet. With a burst of shimmering sparkles, a purple flower appeared. She had earned her fourth charm! Now she was definitely well on her way to becoming a Lucky Star!

Cassie smiled to herself. *I wonder what magic powers this charm has,* she thought.

Jacey finally finished signing autographs and came over to join Cassie and Alex. Tossing her long hair over her shoulder, she kicked off her silver sneakers and stood barefoot on the cool sand.

"You made my wish come true!" she said to Cassie. "Is there anything I can do to thank you?"

Cassie looked thoughtful. "Actually, there is something. . . ."

★ ★ ★

Later that afternoon, Cassie and Alex stood on the doorstep of the Fairy Cupcake Bakery. Comet sat next to them, tail wagging, while Jacey stood quietly behind them. Cassie knocked on the door.

Kate's mom opened it and gasped in surprise when she saw Jacey. "Aren't you the girl who sings 'Magic Moments'?" she asked. "My daughter loves that song."

Jacey smiled. "Yes, I am, and thank you."

"Is Kate up for a few visitors?" Cassie asked.

"For you? Of course!" Kate's mom said.

They went upstairs, and Cassie poked her head around the bedroom door. Kate was sitting up in bed, tucked under a quilt with a pretty cupcake pattern on it.

"Cassie!" Kate said, delighted to see her friend. "Hi, Alex. Hi, Comet," she added as they entered.

Cassie gave Kate a gentle hug. "We have a surprise for you."

She grinned as Jacey walked in and Kate's eyes opened wide in disbelief.

Kate gasped. "Are you . . . ?"

"Hi," Jacey said, smiling at Kate. "I heard you couldn't come to the festival, so Cassie thought we could bring the concert to you. You can hear my new Jacey Day Stars sing."

With that, Jacey, Cassie, and Alex launched into the song. Kate clapped in time, joining Alex's rippling sound-wave dance move from her bed.

"And when I need a friendly face,
I know I'll come back to this place.
Starlight shimmering in the sky,
I will be there by and by."

Seeing Kate's happy face made Cassie realize that there were lots of different kinds of magic in the world—and they didn't all

need charms to make them work!

When they finished singing, Kate's mom walked in with a tray full of beautiful cupcakes. As Cassie took a big bite, she noticed a shooting star flash past the window. Stella Starkeeper!

I can't wait for my next magical adventure, Cassie thought. *It's time to make someone else's wish come true!*

Make Your Own!

You can sing a magical tune, just like Cassie
—all you need is a microphone! Here's how
to create one of your very own:

You Need:
- One cardboard paper towel tube
- Foam ball
- Black craft paint
- Paintbrush
- Craft glue
- Rhinestones, ribbon, buttons, or any other accessories you like

1. Start by using the paintbrush to paint your cardboard tube and foam ball black. Make sure they're fully covered, and let them dry.

2. Once your cardboard tube and foam ball are completely dry, use the craft glue to attach the foam ball to one end of the cardboard tube.

3. Decorate your microphone with rhinestones, ribbon, buttons, or any other fun craft accessories you have on hand. These are what make your microphone special and unlike anyone else's!

4. Use the microphone to sing your favorite song. You're ready to be a rock star now, just like Jacey Day!

Can Cassie make another wish come true?

Take a sneak peek at

#4: Wish Upon a Party!

✦ 1 ✦
The Great Fandango

Cassie carried Twinkle downstairs to the dining room. He sat under the table near Cassie's feet while she and Alex ate some soft-boiled eggs and toast.

"I wonder if it will ever stop raining," Cassie said with a sigh.

"Hi," a new voice interrupted. "I think I can make your gray day disappear!"

Surprised, Cassie turned to see who had spoken. A boy stood in the dining room doorway. He was a little taller than Alex and wore a black cape. He gave them a goofy grin. Cassie recognized him as one of the new guests at the bed-and-breakfast.

"Hi!" Cassie said. "I'm Cassie, and this is Alex."

The new boy bowed. His shiny black cape swung around his shoulders, revealing a bright red lining.

"I am The Great Fandango," he announced in a booming voice.

"That's a very unusual name," Alex said, grinning.

"My real name's Marcus Chen," the boy told them, sitting down. "The Great Fandango is my stage name. I chose Fandango because it sounds magical, and Great because that's what I want my tricks to be."

"You're a magician!" Cassie said excitedly.

Marcus nodded proudly.

"I'm going to be a scientist," said Alex.

"Wow," Marcus said, "that's *great*, too."

Cassie and Alex laughed.

"Why do you have your magician's outfit on now?" Alex asked.

"I'm doing a magic show at my cousin Lia's birthday party," Marcus explained. "She's turning five today. I don't see her very often because we live far away, so the magic show is a birthday surprise."

"What a fun idea!" Alex said.

Cassie and Alex grinned at each other. They knew a lot about magic because of the magical adventures they had with the charms on Cassie's bracelet.

"We love magic," Cassie added.

With a flourish, Marcus pulled out a black wand with a white tip. "Then I'll show you my magic tricks," he said.

He turned the bottom half of Alex's empty eggshell upside down on a plate. Then he shook out a clean napkin and carefully covered the empty shell.

As she watched Marcus, Cassie noticed a glimmer of sunshine peeking through the dining-room window. *This could turn out to be a magical day after all*, she thought with a smile.

RAINBOW magic™

There's Magic in Every Series!

The Rainbow Fairies
The Weather Fairies
The Jewel Fairies
The Pet Fairies
The Fun Day Fairies
The Petal Fairies
The Dance Fairies
The Music Fairies
The Sports Fairies
The Party Fairies
The Ocean Fairies
The Night Fairies
The Magical Animal Fairies
The Princess Fairies

Read them all!

■SCHOLASTIC

www.scholastic.com
www.rainbowmagiconline.com

HiT entertainment

RMFAIRY6

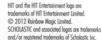